Discovering Cultures

Thailand

Dana Meachen Rau

 **Marshall Cavendish**
Benchmark
New York

For Charlie and Allison

With thanks to Montatip Krishnamra, University of Michigan, Ann Arbor,
for the careful review of this manuscript.

Marshall Cavendish
99 White Plains Road
Tarrytown, New York 10591-9001
www.marshallcavendish.us

Library of Congress Cataloging-in-Publication Data

Rau, Dana Meachen, 1971–
Thailand / by Dana Meachen Rau.
p. cm. — (Discovering cultures)
Includes bibliographical references and index.
ISBN-13: 978-0-7614-1989-1
ISBN-10: 0-7614-1989-6
1. Thailand—Juvenile literature. I. Title. II. Series.
DS563.5.R39 2006
959.3—dc22   2006011475

Photo Research by Candlepants Incorporated
Cover Photo: Dave Bartruff / Corbis

The photographs in this book are used by permission and through the courtesy of: *Photo Researchers Inc.*: Alain Evard, 1, 11; Will & Demi McIntyre, 12, 43(top left). *Corbis*: Chris Lisle, 4, 37; Dave Bartruff, 7, 22; Sukree Sukplang/Reuters, 8, 36(lower); Pierre Schwartz, 9, 44(lower); Free Agents Limited, 14; Jose Fuste Raga, 16, 30; Luca I. Tettoni, 17; Mike McQueen, 18; Kevin R. Morris, 19, 25(lower), 29, 33, 35, back cover; Macduff Everton, 20; Kevin R. Morris, 21; James Marshall, 24; Lindsay hebberd, 25(top); B.S.P.I., 34; Andrea Ryman, 39; Jason Reed/Reuters, 44(top). *Super Stock*: Angelo Cavalli, 6, 42(right). *Peter Arnold Inc.*: Hartmut Schwarzbach, 10, 36(top), 43(lower right), 43(lower left); C. Senanunsakul/UNEP, 13; Chirayut Tolertmongkol/UNEP, 15; Otto Stadler, 31; P.Phukhan-Anant/UNEP, 32. *The Image Works*: Sean Sprague, 26; James Marshall, 28(left). *Getty Images*: Kevin Miller, 27; Hulton Archive/Stringer, 45. *Index Stock*: MedioImages Inc., 28(right); David Marshall, 38.

Cover: *A large Buddha statue at a wat in Thailand*; Title page: *A young Buddhist monk*

Map and illustrations by Ian Warpole
Book design by Virginia Pope

Printed in Malaysia
1 3 5 6 4 2

Turn the Pages...

Where in the World Is Thailand?

*S*a-wat dee! Hello! Welcome to the Kingdom of Thailand. Thailand is in the center of Southeast Asia. This country is a mix of busy cities, working farms, and long held traditions of kings and religion.

The countries surrounding Thailand include Burma in the west and north, Laos in the northeast and east, and Cambodia in the southeast. The southern tip of Thailand is an *isthmus* that separates the Andaman Sea and the Gulf of Thailand. The southern tip of Thailand shares a 314-mile border with Malaysia.

Thailand is divided into four main areas. The north is mountainous and filled with forests. The

Beautiful beaches and thick rain forests dot the isthmus of southern Thailand.

Map of Thailand

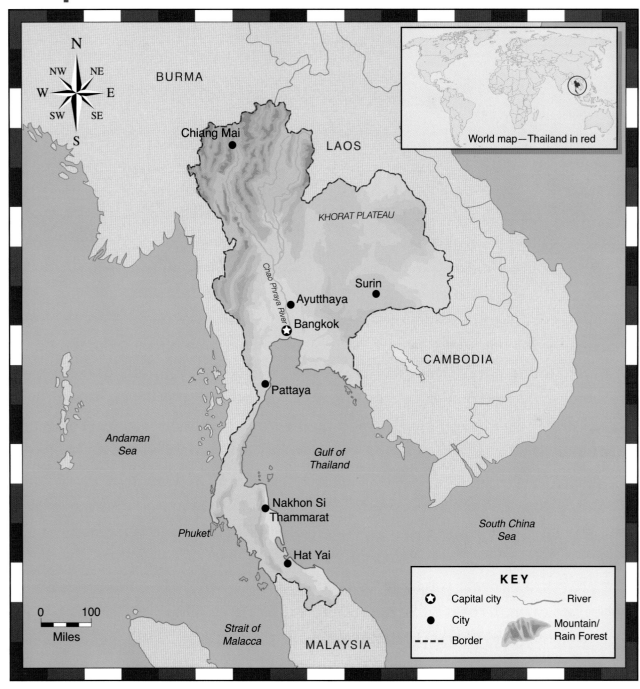

World map—Thailand in red

BURMA

N
NW NE
W E
SW SE
S

Chiang Mai

LAOS

KHORAT PLATEAU

Chao Phraya River

Surin

Ayutthaya

Bangkok

CAMBODIA

Pattaya

Andaman
Sea

Gulf of
Thailand

Nakhon Si
Thammarat

South China
Sea

Phuket

Hat Yai

0   100
Miles

Strait of
Malacca

MALAYSIA

KEY

✪ Capital city   River

● City

- - - Border   Mountain/
                      Rain Forest

Bangkok, Thailand's capital city, lies alongside the Chao Phraya River.

northeast is covered by the Khorat *Plateau*, a high, flat area of land. The long, thin isthmus of the south is dotted with beaches and thick with rain forests. The center of the country, where the most people live, is called the central plain. Here, the Chao Phraya River cuts through the land and makes it rich and fertile for growing many types of crops.

Bangkok, the capital of Thailand, is found in this area. It is the center of business. It is also the center of government and where the king and his family live. Thailand has been led by a king for hundreds of years. The king is the head of the country, and a prime minister runs the government.

Thailand's climate is tropical. Even during its cooler season, the temperature does not go much below 65 degrees Fahrenheit (18 degrees Celsius) in the main parts of Thailand. The mountains of the north are a bit colder, and the rain forests of the isthmus are always hot and humid.

Strong winds, called *monsoons*, bring different seasons to the country. A wet monsoon from the southeast brings Thailand's rainy season from June to October. Though it rains much of the time, the sun still peeks out between showers. Another monsoon arrives in November bringing dry, cooler air. In December and January, the weather is at its coolest. From March to May it is the hottest. Farmers are always eager for the rainy season, which they call *ridu fon*, to start again so their crops get enough water to grow well.

Farmers work hard to produce products that Thailand uses and also trades with other countries. Rice is the main crop. Farmers also grow pineapples, bananas, sugar,

Rice grows in paddies in a field in Thailand.

A worker takes a break at a cement factory.

and coconuts. Because Thailand has such a long coastline, fishing is also important. Rubber and tin are produced in the rain forests of the south. Teakwood is cut down in the forests of the north. Factories make fabric, computers, cement, and furniture.

Ports in Bangkok, and other cities on the coast, welcome incoming ships. Thai ships also leave from these ports to share their goods with other countries in Southeast Asia and the world.

On December 26, 2004, Thailand's southwestern coast was hit with a *tsunami*. This huge wave was caused by an undersea earthquake in the Indian Ocean. Damaging eighteen countries in coastal areas of Asia and Africa, the tsunami killed almost 300,000 people, more than 5,300 in Thailand. Villages, vacation spots, and other buildings were destroyed without warning. Today, the Thai people are still rebuilding after such a devastating event.

Elephant Roundup

Elephants have a history with the Thai people. Long ago, elephants were used in battle and for work. Even today, elephants are still used in the logging business of the north. An elephant is also the symbol of the royal family of Thailand. When you look at a map, you might even agree with many people who think Thailand is shaped like an elephant's head.

Each fall, there is a festival centered around elephants. Surin, a town in the eastern part of Thailand, holds the annual Elephant Roundup. It is like an elephant field day. More than one hundred elephants play soccer, tug-of-war, and run in races. They march in a parade and re-create historic battles. The crowd enjoys watching the strength and intelligence of these incredible beasts. At the end of the parade there is a special elephant breakfast of fruit treats for all the elephants!

What Makes Thailand Thai?

There are almost 65 million people living in Thailand. About 8 million live in the city of Bangkok. Most of the people there, about 75 percent, are Thai. About 14 percent are Chinese. The rest are from Malaysia and other nearby countries. Thailand means "land of the free." The Thai people are very friendly and accepting of others' ideas.

Thai is the national language of Thailand. It is *tonal*, which means that a word can change its meaning depending on the way it is said. English is also spoken throughout Thailand, but especially in the cities.

Almost all Thai people practice Buddhism. Only a small number (about 4 percent) of Malays in the south practice Islam. The religion of Theravada

Almost 95 percent of all Thai people are Buddhist.

These Muslim boys are among the 4 percent of Thai people who practice Islam.

Buddhism in Thailand is based on the teachings of a man named Siddhartha Gautama, known as the Buddha, who lived from 563 BCE to 483 BCE. He devoted his life to peace and goodness. All Buddhist families have a shrine in their homes. A shrine includes small Buddha statues, a pot for burning incense, a vase for fresh flowers, and a pair of candles. In the morning and evening, people pray at the shrine, bowing before it with their foreheads, hands, and knees pressed to the floor.

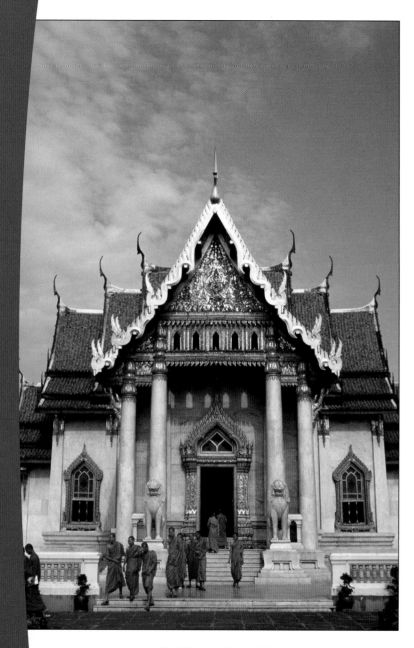

Buddhist monks outside a wat

Buddhists worship at a temple called a *wat*. Wats can be found in every city and village. Monks, who are men who have devoted their lives to Buddhism, live there. The wat also includes a meeting hall and an area for worship. In villages, a wat can be very simple, but nearer to cities, they can be very elaborate. Thailand has more than 30,000 wats.

Thai people wear clothes similar to those worn by people around the world. But when dressing in traditional clothes, a woman might wear a large piece of colorful cloth wrapped around her like a skirt, called a *pha sin*. Men wear pants with a specially designed shirt called a *seua phra ratchathan*. Sashes might be added when they dress up—men wear them around their waists and women wear them over their shoulders.

Thai traditional artwork has very religious themes. Wats are carved with much detail, and are often glistening with gold. Painted murals of the life of the Buddha adorn their inside walls. There are many crafts that have a long history in Thailand. Craftspeople have passed down their skills to others, and many traditional crafts, such as pottery, black *lacquering*, weaving, and silk-making are still practiced today.

On the streets outside a wat, one might see a colorful display of jasmine blossom garlands. People buy these strings of flowers to lay them at the base of a Buddha statue, to present to the king or royal family, or as gifts for friends and family.

One of the traditional forms of entertainment in Thailand is a *khon* performance. This play tells a mythical story called the Ramakien. Narrators tell the story as dancers act out the parts of people, demons, and monkeys. The characters wear

Khon performers in masks and colorful costumes

beautiful masks, as well as very detailed, and often heavy, costumes.

In *lakhon* dancing, women wear pointed headdresses and ornate costumes. They dance barefoot, expressing themselves mostly with their upper body and hands. Some girls start their lakhon training at a very young age.

Likay dancing is more varied than lakhon or khon. Stories can include singing and comedy, and costumes can be traditional or modern. Likay dances are popular at village festivals.

During these shows and dances, music fills the air. In a Thai music group, you might see the large xylophone made of bamboo called the *ranaat ek*. Players might blow a flute called a *pi*. They might pluck the strings of a *so sam sai*. They might keep the beat on a *thon* drum.

A traditional lakhon dancer

14

Shadow Puppets

Nang Talung, a form of puppetry, is a tradition in Thailand that has been practiced for five centuries. Puppets are made out of leather. Then a bright light shines behind them and casts their shadows onto a white sheet. While the audience watches the shadows, puppeteers make the puppets move with long rods.

Living in Thailand

Bangkok began as a small fishing village. It has grown to become the largest city in Thailand. The Silom Road area is where many businesses are located. And Siam Square is where many tourists go shopping. Many Chinese people work and live in

Traffic clogs a busy street in Bangkok.

Thailand's king and his family live in the Grand Palace in Bangkok.

Chinatown. Like many cities, Bangkok is filled with tall skyscrapers. There are also some very poor areas. What makes Bangkok unique are the traditional reminders of the Grand Palace, where the king and his family live, as well as symbols of Buddhism everywhere.

The city of Bangkok is a bustling place. Early in the mornings, the streets fill with traffic, often creating thick smog. People take three-wheeled taxis, called *tuk-tuks*, through the busy streets.

Most Thai people live away from the smog and crowded city. Thailand is a country made up of many villages. These villages are usually clustered along a river

A Buddhist monk rides in the back of a tuk-tuk.

Houses built on stilts sit along the Chao Phraya River north of Bangkok.

or *canal*, called a *klong*. Klongs run all through the farming areas of Thailand, bringing water to crops from the main river. Houses in the villages are built above the ground, on stilts, in case of flooding. The area under the house is a nice shady spot for working on crafts or resting after a hard day. In some villages, houses even float on the water itself. All members of a family may live together in one house, including children, parents, and grandparents.

Most farmers keep water buffalo to help with the farmwork.

In the central part of Thailand, the rice farmers work their fields all day. Most farming families own water buffalo. The buffalo plow the fields and haul heavy loads much better than a tractor could. In the mountainous north, where hill tribes live, they grow some crops, but also raise livestock.

Since rice, or *kaao*, is an important crop in Thailand, it is eaten with every meal —breakfast, lunch, dinner, snacks, and even as dessert. Thai people also love to use spices and herbs. They cook with lemongrass, black pepper, lime, shallots, garlic, coriander, ginger, peanuts, and coconut milk. Chili peppers are what make many Thai dishes very spicy. They come large and small, yellow, red, orange, and green.

Herbs and spices are ground together and made into a paste called a *curry*. The spices are combined with meat, such as beef, lamb, pork, chicken, or duck, as well as seafood, such as fish or shrimp. Vegetables, such as bamboo shoots, cabbage, water chestnuts, and eggplant, are added. Many Thai dishes are either steamed, grilled, or stir-fried to mix the flavors together. Everything is cut up into small, bite-sized pieces, so there is no need for a knife. The meat and vegetables sit on top of rice, or sometimes noodles. *Pad Thai* is a very popular noodle dish all over the world.

Often a Thai table is covered with many bowls. That is because Thai people love to add even more flavor to their dishes. A main meal is sometimes grilled meat and a variety of dipping sauces. The sauces are made with fish sauce or shrimp paste with spices added.

A basket of chili peppers for sale at an outdoor market

A Thai meal is a mix of many flavors—salty, sour, sweet, and bitter. Soups, salads, and main dishes are placed on the table at the same time so that their many flavors can combine. Meals are often shared by more than one person as they sample a taste of each dish. Dessert is almost always sweet after such a spicy meal. Dessert might be fresh fruit, such as mangoes, melons, bananas, pineapples, papayas, or durians, which are prickly on the outside, but creamy and sweet on the inside.

In the busyness of daily life, people can also get meals on the go. Vendors at fast-food stalls sell shoppers almost anything to eat. For breakfast, a Thai person might get *pla tong go*, which are small bits of fried dough, or *khao tom*, a rice soup. For lunch, one might stop at a noodle shop. Here they can buy noodles and add their own spices. They might even stop for a dessert, such as coconut rice and mangoes.

A chef serves a Thai noodle bowl, along with several spices and sauces.

Khao Neow Ma-Muang
(Sticky Rice with Mangoes)

A popular dessert found all over Thailand, especially at outdoor markets, is sticky coconut rice with mangoes.

Ingredients:

1 cup sticky rice
(or jasmine rice)

3/4 cup canned coconut milk

1 1/2 tablespoons sugar

Tiny pinch of salt

1 ripe mango

Sesame seeds (optional)

Banana leaf (optional)

Soak the rice for two hours or more in a bowl of cold water. Then drain and put in saucepan. Add the coconut milk, sugar, salt, and 3/4 cup of water. Bring to a boil and then lower the heat. Keep the saucepan uncovered and simmer for about 7 to 9 minutes or until there is no more liquid, stirring often. Put the cover back on and let it sit for about 10 minutes. Spoon the rice into a double boiler or steamer. Add water to the bottom and bring it to a boil. Steam the rice for about 20 minutes, until the rice is no longer crunchy.

Place a banana leaf on each plate. When the rice is cool, spoon it in a ball-shape onto the leaves. Sprinkle the top of the rice with sesame seeds. Next to the rice, place slices of sweet, fresh mango.

This recipe makes about 3 to 4 servings.

School Days

Just like in your home, Monday to Friday is a busy time for Thai families. Children must get dressed, pack their homework, eat a quick breakfast and then head off to school for a day of learning. Each morning at school, children wearing their uniforms line up to hear the Thai national anthem before they begin classes. Religion is a very important part of the school day. Students take a moment to chant and pray, holding their hands pressed together in a gesture called a *wai*.

Before classes begin, a school band plays Thailand's national anthem.

The Thai people greatly value education. More than 90 percent of Thai people can read and write. All children in Thailand must go to school from the ages of six to fifteen. Public schools are run by the government. There are also a number of private schools in Thailand. Some are connected to a certain group, such as the religious or Chinese schools.

Children read at a school built by the government.

Many Thai children go to preschool, where they learn basic skills, like sharing and how to respect others, as well as play games. Then at age six, they start primary school. Primary school, or the *pràthõm* level, lasts for six years. The children learn math, science, history, geography, and language, as well as English and many other subjects.

Next, students attend secondary school. During the first three years, called the *mátháyom* level, all students continue to learn the same subjects and skills. The next three years, called the *udom*, or high school level, separates

Schoolgirls in uniform laugh together in an auditorium.

25

students into two groups. One group studies subjects that will put them on a path toward attending a university. The other group learns skills to use in the working world, such as farming.

After secondary school, students have a choice. They can begin working if they need to help support their family. Or they can attend a university to continue their studies. Many Thais go to vocational schools that teach them skills for a specific job. There are medical schools, military schools, teacher colleges, and science and research institutes, as well as universities devoted to the Buddhist religion, often attended by monks. Chulalongkorn University was the first university established in Thailand, named after King Chulalongkorn (1853–1910). The *acharns*, or teachers, at a university are highly respected people in Thailand.

A Buddhist monk attends an English class at a wat.

Learning at a Wat

Historically, education was centered around the wat in every community. The monks were the teachers, and most education was focused around teaching and meditating about Buddhism.

Today, most education is conducted in schools, although many schools are still found within the grounds of temples. In more rural areas, where there is little money for schools, the wat is still the central place of instruction for children.

The wat still plays an important role in educating young boys. Thai men are all expected to become monks for about three months at some time in their lives. They help the monks and live like them. It helps their faith grow stronger.

Temple boys go out with the monks to collect food and money. They prepare meals for them and keep the temple clean. They must do as the monks do—shave the hair from their heads and wear saffron robes.

Just for Fun

Three brothers in their front yard

Having fun is an important part of Thai life. The word for fun in Thai is *sanùk*. When a Thai family is not at work or school, they might read the newspaper, listen to the radio, watch television, or surf the Internet. They might shop at malls, stores, or in one of the many floating markets —where people sell their goods from boats in the canal.

Shoppers row through a floating market in Bangkok.

Children explore the ruins of a wat in Ayutthaya.

In their own country, there are many sights to see. A Thai family might visit the ancient city of Ayutthaya, just north of Bangkok. Ayutthaya was the capital of Thailand (then known as Siam) for more than 400 years, from 1350 until 1767. It had once been a great city, where many kings ruled. Today the ruins of the palace, temples, and other buildings are still a grand sight.

Other Thai people might visit an amusement park for the day. Or they might vacation in the south, on the island of Phuket or the beaches of Pattaya. Coral reefs are filled with many types of colorful fish, and scuba divers, sailors, and fishermen have a fun time exploring the wonders underwater.

Thai people and tourists alike enjoy sunbathing and swimming along Thailand's beautiful beaches.

Muay Thai fighters

Many Thai people play sports. Modern sports, such as golf, tennis, rugby, and soccer, attract many players and spectators. Some traditional sports, such as a type of boxing called *Muay Thai*, are a grand spectacle. Unlike today's boxing, traditional Thai boxers can use all parts of their bodies, except for their heads, to punch and kick their opponents. All of the movements are very fast. Before a match begins, there is dancing and music to pay respect to the trainers. Pi pipes, drums, and cymbals play a traditional tune.

Ta-kraw is another fun sport from long ago still played today. The ball is made of wicker and is hollow in the center. Players form a circle and must keep the ball in the air. But they cannot use their hands. They use their heads, feet, elbows, and knees. Some players can perform amazing tricks.

Races on waterways in longboats are also held every year. The boats are made from carved-out tree trunks. Up to fifty oarsmen fill the boats and try to lead their team to victory.

Longboats on the Chao Phraya River

Kite-Flying

In Thailand, kite-flying is not just a fun pastime for children on a windy day. It is a serious and competitive sport. Two types of kites are used. The female kite is called the *pakpao*, and the male kite is the *chula*. The pakpao's small diamond shape helps it dart quickly through the sky. The star-shaped chula is double the size and takes many people to fly.

Kite competitions feature four pakpaos fighting against one chula, with a team of kite-flyers for each kite. The players try to knock each other's kites down using bamboo hooks and shards of glass, and snare other kites with long cloth tails and loops of string.

Let's Celebrate!

The Thai people have many holidays and chances for celebration. Almost every month is marked by an official traditional or religious holiday. The wat is often a center for events. Thai people go to the temple on important days of their lives, such as their birthdays, and holidays that honor Buddha.

In April, the Thai people hold a New Year celebration called Songkran. It lasts for three days, from the thirteenth to the fifteenth, and is a very happy holiday. The night before the holiday begins, people clean their houses

Schoolboys walk past a wat in observance of Buddha's birthday.

34

from top to bottom. They throw away and even burn things they do not need. Worn out items are considered bad luck, and they get rid of them before the new year begins.

The morning of the thirteenth begins with the sound of firecrackers. Families dress in new clothes and visit their local wat. They bring food to the monks. Later in the day, there is a special ceremony where the Buddha statues are bathed. Young children also pour water into the hands of their parents for their blessing.

During the holiday, there are parades, music, and other religious ceremonies, including the Bangsakun to

The winner of a junior beauty contest held during the Songkran Festival

Friends have fun getting soaked with water during a Songkran celebration.

remember those who have died. People also release fish into rivers and caged birds back into the air. One of the most fun parts of the holiday, loved especially by the young, is water-throwing. Just like the other traditions of washing away the past year, throwing water is like giving everyone a bath— even while they are driving down the street! They spray each other with hoses, splash in the rivers, and throw water at each other by the bucketful.

A boy and his elephant spray water at people celebrating the Songkran Festival.

Prayer and meditation are an important part of Magha Puja Day.

Many religious holidays are also celebrated in Thailand. On the day of the first full moon in February, Thai people celebrate Magha Puja Day. It is a day set aside to remember when Buddha preached to 1,250 monks from many different places, who gathered together to hear his teachings. Everyone has a day off from work and school so that they can visit wats and participate in the activities. During the day, people meditate and honor Buddha, and at night, they take part in the Wien Tien procession, walking around the wat holding candles. The king leads the ceremonies at the Wat Phra Kaew, or temple of the Emerald Buddha, in Bangkok. He also leads the candlelit procession around the wat.

Another national holiday special to the Thai people is the celebration of the King's Birthday, also called National Day or Father's Day, on December 5. Born in 1927, King Bhumibol Adulyadej is the longest-reigning monarch in the history of Thailand. The people of Thailand love and respect him. The king, in return, cares much for the people of Thailand, and he is always eager to listen to their needs and to try to make life better for them. To honor this great man, people decorate their homes and businesses with flags and pictures of the king. They pray for him and their country.

Soldiers march in a parade in celebration of the King's Birthday.

Sand Pagodas

Songkran, the Thai New Year celebration, is a fun festival for all—especially children. One event of the holiday is building sand pagodas, or sand castles. The Thai call them *phrasai*. Piles of sand are taken to the grounds of the wat. With special bowls, people gather sand to build a pagoda. Inside the pagoda, they hide a coin and a fig leaf. They decorate their pagodas with flowers, candles, and joss sticks, which are colorfully decorated prayer sticks sold for the occasion.

The trirong, or Thai flag, has three colors. Red symbolizes the country, white is for Buddhism, and blue stands for the monarchy. Five stripes run horizontally, with red stripes on the top and bottom, white stripes next, and one larger blue stripe through the middle.

Thai currency is called the baht. One baht equals 100 satang. There are paper bills of 20, 50, 100, 500, and 1,000 baht that are each a different color and size. There are also coins for 25 and 50 satang, and 1, 5, and 10 baht. In May 2006, one U.S. dollar equaled about 38 baht.

Count in Thai

English	Thai	Say it like this:
one	neung	neung
two	song	sawng
three	saam	saam
four	see	see
five	haah	haah
six	hoke	hoke
seven	jed	jed
eight	pat	paed
nine	gao	gow
ten	sib	sib

Glossary

canal (kuh-NAL)   A man-made waterway.

curry (KUHR-ee)   A paste made from ground herbs and spices.

isthmus (IS-mus)   A very thin piece of land that connects two larger areas of land.

lacquering (LAK-uhr-ing)   A type of wooden artwork where layers of a liquid coating create a glossy finish.

monsoons (mahn-SOONS)   Strong winds that blow at specific times every year.

plateau (pla-TOH)   A high, flat area of land.

tonal (TOH-nuhl)   Said differently to change meaning.

tsunami (soo-NAH-mee)   A huge wave caused by an earthquake.

wat   A Buddhist temple and gathering place.

Fast Facts

Thailand has been led by a king for hundreds of years. The king is the head of the country, and a prime minister runs the government.

KHORAT PLATEAU

Chiang Mai

Chao Phraya River

Surin

Ayutthaya

Bangkok

Pattaya

Nakhon Si Thammarat

Phuket

Hat Yai

Thailand is divided into four main areas: the northern mountains and forests; the Khorat Plateau in the northeast; the long, thin isthmus of beaches and rain forests in the south; and the central plain.

Bangkok, the capital of Thailand, is found in the central plain. Bangkok is the center of Thailand's business and government.

Thailand's climate is tropical. Even during its cooler season, the temperature does not go much below 65 °F (18 °C) in the main parts of Thailand.

The trirong, or Thai flag, has three colors. Red symbolizes the country, white is for Buddhism, and blue stands for the monarchy.

In Thailand, 94.6 percent of the people are Buddhist, 4.6 percent are Muslim, and less than 1 percent are Christian or other religions.

Thai currency is called the baht. One baht equals 100 satang. In May 2006, one U.S. dollar equaled about 38 baht.

Thai is the national language of Thailand. It is tonal, which means that a word can change its meaning depending on the way it is said.

Thailand means "land of the free." The Thai people are very friendly and accepting of others' ideas.

As of July 2006, there were 64,631,595 people living in Thailand. Of that number, 75 percent are Thai, 14 percent are Chinese, and 11 percent are from other backgrounds.

Proud to Be Thai

King Bhumibol Adulyadej (1927–)

King Bhumibol Adulyadej is the ninth king of the Chakri Dynasty in Thailand. Born in Massachusetts while his father was studying medicine at Harvard, he became king of Thailand when he was nineteen. He is the longest-reigning king of Thailand, starting his rule on the throne in 1946. Since then, he has always been deeply respected by the Thai people, who refer to him as "His Majesty." The king has always been very concerned about the welfare of everyone in Thailand, especially the poor in rural areas. Thousands of people come out to greet him when he travels around the country. His birthday is a national holiday.

Sangduen Chailert (1961–)

Elephants have been important to Thai people throughout their history. But for Sangduen Chailert (nicknamed "Lek") they are especially important. Lek was born in a mountain village in Baan Lao and grew up with an elephant that helped her grandfather with farming chores. Ever since, she has wanted to help save Asian elephants as their natural habitats are destroyed by loggers. Lek founded Elephant Nature Park north of Chiang Mai as well as Elephant Haven, where she and her staff help elephants that have been hurt by their owners or in the wild, and then let them live safely in a forest refuge. Lek gives many talks to schoolchildren, and others, about elephant conservation.

Chang and Eng (1811–1874)

These world-famous brothers, born near Bangkok, in Siam, were known because of the way they were born—joined at the chest. They tried to lead a normal life as children, fishing with their father. As they grew older, they traveled the world showing themselves off as a curiosity. Tired of life on display, they settled in the United States in North Carolina, where they ran a shop, lived on a farm, married two sisters, and had several children apiece.

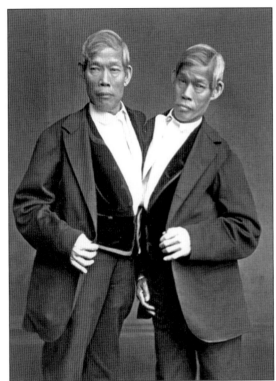

Find Out More

Books

Countries and Cultures: Thailand by Tracey Boraas. Bridgestone Books, 2002.

Countries of the World: Thailand by Ronald Cherry. Gareth Stevens Publishing, 2000.

Muay Thai: Thai Boxing by Paul Collins. Chelsea House Publications, 2001.

World of Recipes: Thailand by Sue Townsend. Heinemann Library, 2002.

Web Sites*

www.odci.gov/cia/publications/factbook/geos/th.html

The World Factbook lists all the important facts about Thailand, with information about the land, people, government, and business.

http://thaiembdc.org

The Web site of the *Royal Thai Embassy* in Washington, D.C., is filled with a lot of general information about Thailand and its people.

www1.thaimain.org/en/

Thailand's Official Information Center is filled with facts about Thailand, its food, people, government, and traditions.

*All Internet sites were available and accurate when sent to press.

Index

Page numbers for illustrations are in **boldface.**

About the Author

Dana Meachen Rau is an author, editor, and illustrator. A graduate of Trinity College in Hartford, Connecticut, she has written more than one hundred books for children, including nonfiction, biographies, early readers, and historical fiction. She lives and works in Burlington, Connecticut, with her husband, Chris, and children, Charlie and Allison.